BLUE-BIRD
WEATHER

BLUE-BIRD WEATHER

ROBERT W. CHAMBERS

WILDSIDE PRESS

BLUE-BIRD WEATHER

Published in 2007 by Wildside Press.
www.wildsidepress.com

I

It was now almost too dark to distinguish objects; duskier and vaguer became the flat world of marshes, set here and there with cypress and bounded only by far horizons; and at last land and water disappeared behind the gathered curtains of the night. There was no sound from the waste except the wind among the withered reeds and the furrowing splash of wheel and hoof over the submerged causeway.

The boy who was driving had scarcely spoken since he strapped Marche's gun cases and valise to the rear of the rickety wagon at the railroad station. Marche, too, remained silent, preoccupied with his own reflections. Wrapped in his fur-lined coat, arms folded, he sat doubled forward, feeling the Southern swamp-chill busy with his bones. Now and then he was obliged to relight his pipe, but the cold bit at his fingers, and he hurried to protect himself again with heavy gloves.

The small, rough hands of the boy who was driving were naked, and finally Marche mentioned it, asking the child if he were not cold.

"No, sir," he said, with a colorless brevity that might have been shyness or merely the dull indifference of the very poor, accustomed to discomfort.

"Don't you feel cold at all?" persisted Marche kindly.

"No, sir."

"I suppose you are hardened to this sort of weather?"

"Yes, sir."

By the light of a flaming match, Marche glanced sideways at him as he drew his pipe into a glow once more, and for an instant the boy's gray eyes flickered toward his in the flaring light. Then darkness masked them both again.

"Are you Mr. Herold's son?" inquired the young man.

"Yes, sir," almost sullenly.

"How old are you?"

"Eleven."

"You're a big boy, all right. I have never seen your father. He is at the clubhouse, no doubt."

"Yes, sir," scarcely audible.

"And you and he live there all alone, I suppose?"

"Yes, sir." A moment later the boy added jerkily, "And my sister," as though truth had given him a sudden nudge.

"Oh, you have a sister, too?"

"Yes, sir."

"That makes it very jolly for you, I fancy," said Marche pleasantly. There was no reply to the indirect question.

His pipe had gone out again, and he knocked the ashes from it and pocketed it. For a while they drove on in silence, then Marche peered impatiently through the darkness, right and left, in an effort to see; and gave it up.

"You must know this road pretty well to be able to keep it," he said. "As for me, I can't see anything except a dirty little gray star up aloft."

"The horse knows the road."

"I'm glad of that. Have you any idea how near we are to the house?"

"Half a mile. That's Rattler Creek, yonder."

"How the dickens can you tell?" asked Marche curiously. "You can't see anything in the dark, can you?"

"I don't know how I can tell," said the boy indifferently.

Marche smiled. "A sixth sense, probably. What did you say your name is?"

"Jim."

"And you're eleven? You'll be old enough to have a gun very soon, Jim. How would you like to shoot a real, live wild duck?"

"I *have* shot plenty."

Marche laughed. "Good for you, Jimmy. What did the gun do to you? Kick you flat on your back?"

The boy said gravely: "Father's gun is too big for me. I have to rest it on the edge of the blind when I fire."

"Do you shoot from the blinds?"

"Yes, sir."

Marche relapsed into smiling silence. In a few moments he was thinking of other things — of this muddy island which had once been the property of a club consisting of five carefully selected and wealthy members, and which, through death and resignation, had now reverted to him. Why he had ever bought in the shares, as one by one the other members either died or dropped out, he did not exactly know. He didn't care very much for duck shooting. In five years he had not visited the club; and why he had come here this year for a week's sport he scarcely knew, except that he had either to go somewhere for a rest or ultimately be carried, kicking, into what his slangy doctor called the "funny house."

So here he was, on a cold February night, and already nearly at his destination; for now he could make out a light across the marsh, and from dark and infinite distances the east wind bore the solemn rumor of the sea, muttering of wrecks and death along the Atlantic sands beyond the inland sounds.

"Well, Jim," he said, "I never thought I'd survive this drive, but here we are, and still alive. Are you frozen solid, you poor boy?"

The boy smiled, shyly, in negation, as they drove into the bar of light from the kitchen window and stopped. Marche got down very stiffly. The kitchen door opened at the same moment, and a woman's figure appeared in the lamplight — a young girl, slender, bare armed, drying her fingers as she came down the steps to offer a small, weather-roughened hand to Marche.

"My brother will show you to your room," she said. "Supper will be ready in a few minutes."

So he thanked her and went away with Jim, relieving the boy of the valise and one gun-case, and presently came to the quarters prepared for him. The room was rough, with its unceiled walls of yellow pine, a chair, washstand, bed, and a nail or two for his wardrobe. It had been the affectation of the wealthy men composing the Foam Island Duck Club to exist almost primitively when on the business of duck shooting, in contradistinction to the overfed luxury of other millionaires inhabiting other more luxuriously appointed shooting-boxes along the Chesapeake.

The Foam Island Club went in heavily for simplicity, as far as the two-story shanty of a clubhouse was concerned; but their island was one of the most desirable in the entire region, and their live decoys the most perfectly trained and cared for.

Marche, washing his tingling fingers and visage in icy water, rather wished, for a moment, that the club had installed modern plumbing; but delectable odors from the kitchen put him into better humor, and presently he went off down the creaking and unpainted stairs to warm himself at a big stove until summoned to the table.

He was summoned in a few moments by the same girl who had greeted him; and she also waited on him at table, placing before him in turn his steaming soup, a platter of fried bass and smoking sweet potatoes, then the inevitable broiled canvas-back duck with rice, and finally home-made pre-serves — wild grapes, exquisitely fragrant in their thin, golden syrup.

Marche was that kind of a friendly young man who is nat-urally gay-hearted and also a little curious — sometimes to the verge of indiscretion. For his curiosity and inquiring interest in his fellow-men was easily aroused — particularly when they were less fortunately situated than he in a world where it is a favorite fiction that all are created equal. He was, in fact, that particular species of human nuisance known as a humanitarian; but he never dreamed he was a nuisance, and certainly never meant to be.

Warmth and food and the prospects of tomorrow's shooting, and a slender, low-voiced young girl, made cheerful his recently frost-nipped soul, and he was inclined to expand and become talkative there in the lamplight.

"Has the shooting been pretty good?" he asked pleasantly, plying knife and fork in the service of a raging appetite.

"It *has* been."

"What do you think of the prospects for tomorrow?"

She said gravely: "I am afraid it will be blue-bird weather."

It was a new, but graphic, expression to him; and he often remembered it afterward, and how quaintly it fell from her lips as she stood there in the light of the kerosene lamp, slim, self-possessed, in her faded gingham gown and apron, the shapely middle finger of one little weather-tanned hand resting on the edge of the cloth.

"You are Miss Herold, I suppose?" he said, looking up at her with his pleasant smile.

"Yes."

"You are not Southern?"

"No," she said briefly. And he then remembered that the Hon. Cicero W. Gilkins, when he was president of the now defunct club, had installed a Northern man as resident chief game-protector and superintendent at the Foam Island Club House.

Marche had never even seen Herold; but, through lack of personal interest, and also because he needed somebody to look out for the property, he had continued to pay this man Herold his inconsiderable salary every year, scarcely knowing, himself, why he did not put the Foam Island shooting on the market and close up the matter for good.

"It's been five years since I was here, Miss Herold," he said, smiling. "That was in the old days of the club, when Judge Gilkins and Colonel Vyse used to come here shooting every season. But you don't remember them, I fancy."

"I remember them."

"Really! You must have been quite a child."

"I was thirteen."

"Oh, then you are eighteen, now," he said humorously.

Her grave, young lips were only slightly responsive to his smile.

"You have been here a long time," he said. "Do you find it lonely?"

"Sometimes," she admitted.

"What do you do for recreation?"

"I don't think I know what you mean, Mr. Marche."

"I mean for pleasure."

She looked at him out of her clear, gray eyes, then turned her gaze on the window. But she could not see through it; the pane only reflected her face darkly; and to her, for a moment, it seemed that way with her whole pent-up life, here in the Virginia marshes — no outlet, no outlook, and wherever she turned her wistful eyes only her own imprisoned self to confront her out of the dull obscurity.

"I suppose," he said, watching her, "that you sometimes go to Norfolk for a holiday?"

"No."

"Or to Old Point, or Baltimore, perhaps?"

She had her under lip between her teeth, now, and was looking so fixedly at the window that he thought she had not heard him.

He rose from the table, and as she turned to meet his pleasant eyes he smilingly thanked her for waiting on him.

"And now," he said, "if you will say to your father that I'd like to have a little talk with him —"

"Father is ill in bed," she said, in a low voice.

"Oh, I'm sorry. I hope it isn't anything serious."

"I — think not."

"Will he be able to see me tomorrow?"

"I am afraid not, Mr. Marche. He — he asked me to say to you that you might safely transact any business with me. I know all about it," she said, speaking a little hurriedly. "I keep the accounts, and I have every item and every bill ready for your inspection; and I can tell you exactly what condition the property is in and what lumber has been cut and what repairs have been necessary. Whenever you are ready for me, I will come into the sitting room," she added, "because Jim and I have had our supper."

"Very well," he said, smiling, "I am ready now, if you are."

So she went away to rinse her hands and lay aside her apron, and in a few minutes she entered the sitting room. He rose and placed a chair for her, and she thanked him, flushing a little, and then he resumed his seat, watching her sorting over the papers in her lap.

Presently she crossed one knee over the other, and one slim, prettily shaped foot, in its shabby shoe, swung clear of its shadow on the floor. Then she handed him a sheaf of bills for his inspection, and, pencil in hand, followed the totals as he read them off aloud.

For half an hour they compared and checked off items, and he found her accounts accurate to a penny.

"Father bought three geese and a gander from Ike Helm," she said. "They were rather expensive, but two were mated, and they call very well when tied out separated. Do you think it was too expensive?" she added timidly, showing him the bill.

"No," he said, smiling. "I think it's all right. Mated decoys are what we need, and you can wing-tip a dozen before you get one that will talk at the right time."

"That is true," she said eagerly. "We try our best to keep up the decoys and have nothing but talkers. Our geese are nearly all right, and our ducks are good, but our swans are *so* vexing! They seem to be such fools, and they usually behave like silly cygnets. You will see tomorrow."

While she was speaking, her brother came quietly into the room with an open book in his hands, and Marche, glancing at it curiously, saw that it was a Latin grammar.

"Where do you go to school, Jim?" he asked.

"Father teaches me."

Marche, rather astonished at the calibre of his superintendent, glanced from the boy to his sister in silence. The girl's head remained steadily lowered over the papers on her knee, but he saw her foot swinging in nervous rhythm, and he was conscious of her silent impatience at something or other, perhaps at the interruption in their business discussion.

"Well," he said pleasantly, "what comes next, Miss Herold?"

She handed him a list of the decoys. He read it gravely, nodded, and returned it.

"You may count them for yourself tomorrow," she said.

"Not at all. I trust you entirely," he replied laughingly.

Then they went over the remaining matters, the condition of the pine timber, the repairs to the boats and blinds and stools, items for snaps, swivels, paint, cement, wire, none of which interested Marche as much as the silent boy reading his Latin grammar by the smoky lamp interested him, or the boy's sister bending over the papers on her knee, pencil poised in her pretty, weather-roughened hand.

"I sent the shells from New York by express," he said. "Did they arrive?"

"I left two hundred in your room," said the boy, looking up.

"Oh, thank you, Jim." And, turning to his sister, who had raised her head, inquiringly, "I suppose somebody will call me at the screech of dawn, won't they?"

"Do you know the new law?" she asked.

"No. I don't like laws, anyway," he said smilingly.

She smiled, too, gathering up her papers preparatory to departure. "Nobody is allowed," she said, "to put off from shore until the sun is above the horizon line. And the wardens are very strict." Then she rose. "Will you excuse me? I have the dishes to do."

The boy laid aside his book and stood up, but his sister said:

"Stay and study, Jim. I don't need any help."

And Jim resumed his seat with heightened color. A moment later, however, he went out to the kitchen.

"Look here, Molly," he said, "wha'd' you want to give me away for? He'll think I'm a sissy, helping you do dishes and things."

"My dear, my dear!" she exclaimed contritely, "I didn't think of it. Please forgive me, Jim. Anyway, you don't really care what this man thinks about any of us —"

"Yes, I do! Anyway, a fellow doesn't want another fellow to think he washes dishes."

"You darling! Forgive me. I wasn't thinking. It was too stupid of me."

"It really was," said the boy, in his sweet, dignified voice, "and I'd been telling him that I'd shot ducks, too."

His sister caught him around the neck and kissed his blonde head. "I'm *so* sorry, Jim. He won't think of it again. If he does, he'll only respect a boy who is so good to his sister. And," she added, cautioning him with lifted finger, "don't talk too much to him, Jim, no matter how nice and kind he is. I know how lonely you are and how pleasant it is to talk to a man like Mr. Marche; but remember that father doesn't wish us to say anything about ourselves or about him, so we must be careful."

"Why doesn't father want us to speak about him or ourselves to Mr. Marche?" asked the boy.

His sister had gone back to her dishes. Now, looking around over her shoulder, she said seriously, "That is father's affair, dear, not ours."

"But don't you know why?"

"Shame on you, Jim! What father cares to tell us he will tell us; but it's exceedingly bad manners to ask."

"Is father really very ill?"

"I told you that to ask me such things is improper," said the girl, coloring. "He has told us that he does not feel well, and that he prefers to remain in his room for a few days. That is enough for us, isn't it?"

"Yes," said the boy thoughtfully.

II

Marche, buried under a mountain of bed clothes, dreamed that people were rapping noisily on his door, and grinned in his dream, meaning to let them rap until they tired of it. Suddenly a voice sounded through his defiant slumbers, clear and charming as a golden ray parting thick clouds. The next moment he found himself awake, bolt upright in the icy dusk of his room, listening.

"Mr. Marche! Won't you *please* wake up and answer?" came the clear, young voice again.

"I *beg* your pardon!" he cried. "I'll be down in a minute!"

He heard her going away downstairs, and for a few seconds he squatted there, huddled in coverings to the chin, and eying the darkness in a sort of despair. The feverish drive of Wall Street, late suppers, and too much good fellowship had not physically hardened Marche. He was accustomed to have his bath tempered comfortably for his particular brand of physique. Breakfast, also, was a most carefully ordered informality with him.

The bitter chill smote him. Cursing the simple life, he crawled gingerly out of bed, suffered acutely while hunting for a match, lighted the kerosene lamp with stiffened fingers, and looked about him, shivering. Then, with a suppressed anathema, he stepped into his folding tub and emptied the arctic contents of the water pitcher over himself.

Half an hour later he appeared at the breakfast table, hungrier than he had been in years. There was nobody there to wait on him, but the dishes and coffee pot were piping hot, and he madly ate eggs and razor-back, and drank quantities of coffee, and finally set fire to a cigarette, feeling younger and happier than he had felt for ages.

Of one thing he was excitedly conscious: that dreadful and persistent dragging feeling at the nape of his neck had vanished. It didn't seem possible that it could have disappeared overnight, but it had, for the present, at least.

He went into the sitting room. Nobody was there, either, so he broke his sealed shell boxes, filled his case with sixes and fives and double B's, drew his expensive ducking gun from its case and took a look at it, buckled the straps of his hip boots to his belt, felt in the various pockets of his shooting coat to see whether matches, pipe, tobacco, vaseline, oil, shell extractor, knife, handkerchief, gloves, were in their proper places; found them so, and, lighting another cigarette, strolled contentedly around the small and almost bare room, bestowing a contented and patronizing glance upon each humble article and decoration as he passed.

Evidently this photograph, in an oval frame of old-time water gilt, was a portrait of Miss Herold's mother. What a charming face, with its delicate, high-bred nose and lips! The boy, Jim, had her mouth and nose, and his sister her eyes, slightly tilted to a slant at the outer corners — beautifully shaped eyes, he remembered.

He lingered a moment, then strolled on, viewing with tolerant indifference the few poor ornaments on the mantel, the chromos of wild ducks and shore birds, and found himself again by the lamp-lit table from which he had started his explorations.

On it were Jim's Latin book, a Bible, and several last year's magazines.

Idly he turned the flyleaf of the schoolbook. Written there was the boy's name — "Jim, from Daddy."

As he was closing the cover a sudden instinct arrested his hand, and, not knowing exactly why, he reopened the book and read the inscription again. He read it again, too, with a vague sensation of familiarity with it, or with the book, or something somehow connected with it, he could not tell exactly what; but a slightly uncomfortable feeling remained as he laid aside the book and stood with brows knitted and eyes absently bent on the stove.

The next moment Jim came in, wearing a faded overcoat which he had outgrown.

"Hello!" said Marche, looking up. "Are you ready for me,

Jim?"

"Yes, sir."

"What sort of a chance have I?"

"I'm afraid it is blue-bird weather," said the boy diffidently.

Marche scowled, then smiled. "Your sister said it would probably be that kind of weather. Well, we all have to take a sporting chance with things in general, don't we, Jim?"

"Yes, sir."

Marche picked up his gun case and cartridge box. The boy offered to take them, but the young man shook his head.

"Lead on, old sport!" he said cheerily. "I'm a beast of more burdens than you know anything about. How's your father, by the way?"

"I think father is about the same."

"Doesn't he need a doctor?"

"No, sir, I think not."

"What is it, Jim? Fever?"

"I don't know," said the boy, in a low voice. He led the way, and Marche followed him out of doors.

A gray light made plain the desolation of the scene, although the sun had not yet risen. To the south and west the sombre pine woods stretched away; eastward, a few last year's cornstalks stood, withered in the clearing, through which a rutted road ran down to the water.

"It isn't the finest farming land in the world, is it, Jim?" he said humorously.

"I haven't seen any other land," said the boy quietly.

"Don't you remember the Northern country at all?"

"No, sir — except Central Park."

"Oh, you were New-Yorkers?"

"Yes, sir. Father —" and he fell abruptly silent.

They were walking together down the rutted road, and Marche glanced around at him.

"What were you going to say about your father, Jim?"

"Nothing." Then truth jogged his arm. "I mean I was only going to say that father and mother and all of us lived there."

"In New York?"

"Yes, sir."

"Is your — your mother living?"

"No, sir."

"I think I saw her picture in the sitting room," he said gently. "She must have been everything a mother should be."

"Yes, sir."

"Was it long ago, Jim?"

"When she died?"

"Yes."

"Yes, very long ago. Six years ago."

"Before you came here, then?"

"Yes, sir."

After they had walked in silence for a little while, Marche said, "I suppose you have arranged for somebody to take me out?"

"Yes, sir."

They emerged from the lane to the shore at the same moment, and Marche glanced about for the expected bayman.

"Oh, there he is!" he said, as a figure came from behind a dory and waded leisurely shoreward through the shallows — a slight figure in hip boots and wool shooting hood and coat, who came lightly across the sands to meet him. And, astonished, he looked into the gray eyes of Molly Herold.

"Father could not take you," she said, without embarrassment, "and Jim isn't quite big enough to manage the swans and geese. Do you mind my acting as your bayman?"

"Mind?" he repeated. "No, of course not. Only — it seems rather rough on you. Couldn't you have hired a bayman for me?"

"I will, if you wish," she said, her cheeks reddening. "But, really, if you'll let me, I am perfectly accustomed to bayman's work."

"Do you *want* to do it?"

She said, without self-consciousness, "If it is the same to you, Mr. Marche, I had rather that the bayman's wages came to us."

"Certainly — of course," he said hurriedly. Then, smiling: "You look the part. I took you for a young man, at first. Now, tell me how I can help you."

"Jim can do that. Still, if you don't mind handling the decoys —"

"Not at all," he said, going up to the fenced inclosures which ran from a rod or two inland down into the shallow water, making three separate yards for geese, swans, and ducks.

Jim was already in the duck pen, hustling the several dozen mallard and black ducks into an inland corral. The indignant birds, quacking a concerted protest, waddled up from the shore, and, one by one, the boy seized the suitable ones, and passed them over the fence to Marche. He handed them to Molly Herold, who waded out to the dory, a duck tucked under either arm, and slipped them deftly into the decoy-crates forward and aft.

The geese were harder to manage — great, sleek, pastel-tinted birds whose wing blows had the force of a man's fist — and they flapped and struggled and buffeted Jim till his blonde head spun; but at last Marche and Molly had them crated in the dory.

 Then the wild swans' turn came — great, white creatures with black beaks and feet; and Molly and Marche were laughing as they struggled to catch them and carry them aboard.

But at last every decoy was squatting in the crates; the mast had been stepped, guns laid aboard, luncheon stowed away. Marche set his shoulder to the stern; the girl sprang aboard, and he followed; the triangular sail filled, and the boat glided out into the sound, straight into the glittering lens of the rising sun.

A great winter gull flapped across their bows; in the lee of Starfish Island, long strings of wild ducks rose like shredded clouds, and, swarming in the sky, swinging, drifting, sheered eastward, out toward the unseen Atlantic.

"Bluebills and sprigs," said the girl, resting her elbow on

the tiller. "There are geese on the shoal, yonder. They've come out from Currituck. Oh, I'm afraid it's to be blue-bird weather, Mr. Marche."

"I'm afraid it is," he assented, smiling. "What do you do in that case, Miss Herold?"

"Go to sleep in the blind," she admitted, with a faint smile, the first delicate approach to anything resembling the careless confidence of camaraderie that had yet come from her.

"See the ducks!" she said, as bunch after bunch parted from the water, distantly, yet all around them, and, gathering like clouds of dusky bees, whirled away through the sky until they seemed like bands of smoke high drifting. Presently she turned and looked back, signaling adieu to the shore, where her brother lifted his arm in response, then turned away inland.

"That's a nice boy," said Marche briefly, and glanced up to see in his sister's face the swift and exquisite transformation that requires no words as answer.

"You seem to like him," said he, laughing.

Molly Herold's gray eyes softened; pride, that had made the love in them brilliant, faded until they grew almost sombre. Silent, her aloof gaze remained fixed on the horizon; her lips rested on each other in sensitive curves. There was no sound save the curling of foam under the bows.

Marche looked elsewhere; then looked at her again. She sat motionless, gray eyes remote, one little, wind-roughened hand on the tiller. The steady breeze filled the sail; the dory stood straight away toward the blinding glory of the sunrise.

Through the unreal golden light, raft after raft of wild ducks rose and whirled into the east; blue herons flopped across the water; a silver-headed eagle, low over the waves, winged his way heavily toward some goal, doggedly intent upon his own business.

Outside Starfish Shoal the girl eased the sheet as the wind freshened. Far away on Golden Bar thousands of wild geese, which had been tipping their sterns skyward in plunging quest of nourishment, resumed a more stately and normal posture, as though at a spoken command; and the long ranks, swimming, and led by age and wisdom, slowly moved away into the glittering east.

At last, off the starboard bow, the low, reedy levels of Foam Island came into view, and in a few minutes more the dory lay in the shallows, oars, mast, and rag stowed; and the two young people splashed busily about in their hip boots, carrying guns, ammunition, and food into the blind.

Then Molly Herold, standing on the mud bank, flung, one by one, a squadron of wooden, painted, canvasback decoys into the water, where they righted themselves, and presently rode the waves, bobbing and steering with startling fidelity to the real things.

Then it came the turn of the real things. Marche and Molly, a struggling bird tucked under each arm, waded out along the lanes of stools, feeling about under the icy water until their fingers encountered the wire-cored cords. Then, to the leg rings of each madly flapping duck and swan and goose they snapped on the leads, and the tethered birds, released, beat the water into foam and flapped and splashed and tugged, until, finally reconciled, they began to souse themselves with great content, and either mounted their stools or swam calmly about as far as their tethers permitted.

Marche, struggling knee-deep in the water, his arms full of wildly flapping gander, hailed Molly for instructions.

"That's a mated bird!" she called out to him. "Peg him outside by himself!"

So Marche pegged out the furious old gander, whose name was Uncle Dudley, and in a few minutes that dignified and insulted bird, missing his spouse, began to talk about it.

Every wifely feeling outraged, his spouse replied loudly from the extreme end of the inner lane, telling her husband, and every duck, goose, and swan in the vicinity, what she thought of such an inhuman separation.

Molly laughed, and so did Marche. Duck after duck, goose after goose, joined indignantly in the conversation. The mallard drakes twisted their emerald-green heads and began that low, half gurgling, half quacking conversation in which their mottled brown and gray mates joined with louder quacks. The geese conversed freely; but the long-necked swans held their peace, occupied with the problem of picking to pieces the snaps on their anklets.

"Now," said Molly breathlessly, as the last madly protesting bird had been stooled, "let's get into the blind as soon as we can, Mr. Marche. There may be ducks in Currituck still, and every minute counts now."

So Marche towed the dory around to the westward and drew it into a channel where it might lie concealed under the reeds.

When he came across to the blind he found Molly there, seated on the plank in the cemented pit behind the screen of reeds and rushes, laying out for him his cartridges.

There they were, in neat rows on the rail, fives, sixes, and a few of swanshot, ranged in front of him. And his 12-gauge, all ready, save for the loading, lay across the pit to his right. So he dropped his booted feet into the wooden tub where a foot-warmer lay, picked up the gun, slid a pair of sixes into it, laid it beside him, and turned toward Miss Herold.

The wool collar of her sweater was turned up about her delicately molded throat and face. The wild-rose color ran riot in her cheeks, and her eyes, sky tinted now, were wide open under the dark lashes, and the wind stirred her hair till it rippled bronze and gold under the edge of her shooting hood. She, too, was perfectly ready. A cheap, heavy, and rather rusty gun lay beside her; a heap of cheap cartridges before her.

She turned, and, catching Marche's eyes, smiled adorably, with a slight nod of comradeship. Then, the smile still faintly curving her lips, she crossed her legs in the pit, and, warming her hands in the pockets of her coat, leaned back, resting against the rail behind.

"You haven't a foot-warmer," he said.

"I'm not cold — only my fingers — a little — stooling those birds."

They spoke in low voices, under their breath.

He fished from his pocket a flat Japanese hand-warmer, lighted the paper-cased punk, snapped it shut, and passed it to her. But she demurred.

"You need it yourself."

"No, I'm all right. Please take it."

So she shyly took it, dropped it into her pocket, and rested her shapely little hand on it. "How delightful!" she said presently, shifting it to the other pocket. "Don't you really need it, Mr. Marche?"

"No. Does it warm you?"

"It is delicious. I *was* a little chilled." She drew out one bare hand and looked at it thoughtfully. Then, with a little sigh, and quite unconscious of his gaze, she touched her lips to the wind-roughened skin, as though in atonement for her maltreatment of herself.

Even as it now was the shape and beauty of the hand held Marche fascinated; it was so small, yet so firm and strong and competent, so full of youthful character, such a delicately fashioned little hand, and so pathetic, somehow — this woman's hand, with its fineness of texture and undamaged purity under the chapped and cruelly bruised, tender skin.

She pocketed it again, looking out from under the wind-blown hair clustering from the edge of her shooting hood. "Blue-bird weather," she said, in her low and very sweet voice. "If no birds swing in by ten o'clock we might as well sleep until four."

Marche leaned forward and scanned the water and sky alternately. Nothing stirred, save their lazily preening decoys. Uncle Dudley was still conversing with his wife at intervals; the swans and the cygnets fed or worried their leash snaps; the ducks paddled, or dozed on the stools, balanced on one leg.

Far away, on Golden Bar, half a thousand wild geese floated, feeding; beyond, like snowflakes dotting the water, a few wild swans drifted. There were ducks, too, off Starfish Island again, but nothing flying in the blue except a slow hawk or some wandering gull, or now and then an eagle — sometimes a mature bird, in all the splendor of white head and tail, sometimes a young bird, seemingly larger, and all gray from crest to shank.

Once an eagle threatened the decoys, and Uncle Dudley swore so lustily at him, and every duck and goose set up such a clamor, that Molly Herold picked up her gun for the emergency. But the magnificent eagle, beating up into the wind with bronze wings aglisten, suddenly sheered off; and, as he passed, Marche could see his bold head turn toward the blind where the sun had flashed him its telegraphic warning on the barrel of Molly's lifted gun.

"Fine!" he whispered. "Splendid! I'm glad you didn't kill him."

"I'm glad I didn't have to," she said.

"Do you think you could have?"

She turned toward him, wondering whether he might be serious; then smiled as he smiled.

At the same instant, coming apparently from nowhere, four canvasbacks suddenly appeared over the clamoring decoys, so close in that, as they came driving by the blind and rose slightly, wings bowed, Marche could almost see their beady little eyes set in the chestnut red of the turning heads. Mechanically his gun spoke twice; rap-rap, echoed Miss Herold's gun, and splash! splash! down whirled two gray-and-red ducks; then a third, uncertain, slowed down, far out beyond the decoys, and slanted sideways to the water. The fourth went on.

"Duffer that I am," said Marche good-humoredly. "That was a clean double of yours, Miss Herold! — clean-cut work."

She said, slightly knitting her straight brows: "I should have crossed two of them and killed the one you missed. I think I'd better get the boat."

"No, I'll go out after that kicker," he said, ashamed of his slovenly work.

Five minutes later he returned with his kicker and her two ducks — great, fat, heavy canvasbacks, beautiful in their red, black, and drab plumage.

"What about blue-bird weather, now?" he laughed.

But she only smiled and said, "I'm very much afraid."

For a long while they sat there, alert behind their wall of rustling reeds, watching sky and water. False alarms were not infrequent from their decoys. Sometimes the outbreak of quacking and honking was occasioned by some wandering gull, sometimes by a circling hawk or some eagle loitering in mid-heaven on broad and leisurely wings, reluctant to remain, unwilling to go; sometimes to a pair or two of widgeon or pintails speeding eastward high in the blue. But the sparkling, cloudless hours sped away, and no duck or goose or swan invaded the vicinity. Only one sly old black duck dropped into the reeds far back on the island; and Marche went after him with serious designs upon his fraudulent old life.

When the young man returned, twenty minutes later, perfectly innocent of duck murder, he found the girl curled up in her corner of the pit, eyes closed, tired little head cradled in the curve of her left arm. She waked as he slid into the blind, and smiled at him, pretending not to have been asleep.

"Did you get him?"

"No. He went off at two hundred yards."

"Blue-bird weather," she sighed; and again they exchanged smiles. He noticed that her eyes had somehow become exceedingly blue instead of the clear gray which he had supposed was their color. And, after her brief slumber, there seemed to be a sort of dewy freshness about them, and about her slightly pink cheeks, which, at that time, he had no idea were at all perilous to him. All he was conscious of was a sensation of pleasure in looking at her, and a slight surprise in the revelation of elements in her which, he began to decide, constituted real beauty.

"That's a quaint expression — 'blue-bird weather,'" he said. "It's a perfect description of a spring-like day in winter. Is it a local expression?"

"Yes — I think so. There's a song about it, along the

coast" — she laughed uncertainly — "a rather foolish song."

"What is it?"

"If I remember" — she hesitated, thinking for a moment, then, with a laugh which he thought a little bashful — "it's really too silly to repeat!"

"Please sing it!"

"Very well — if you wish."

And in a low, pretty, half-laughing voice, she sang:

> *"Quiet sea and quiet sky,*
> *Idle sail and anchored boat,*
> *Just a snowflake gull afloat,*
> *Drifting like a feather —*
> *And the gray hawk crying,*
> *And a man's heart sighing —*
> *That is blue-bird weather: —*
> *And the high hawk crying,*
> *And a maid's heart sighing*
> *Till lass and lover come together, —*
> *This is blue-bird weather."*

She turned her head and looked steadily out across the waste of water. "I told you it was silly," she said, very calmly.

III

Blue-bird weather continued. Every day for a week Marche and Molly Herold put out for Foam Island under summer skies, and with a soft wind filling the sail; and in all the water-world there was no visible sign of winter, save the dead reeds on muddy islands and the far and wintry menace of the Atlantic crashing icily beyond the eastern dunes.

Few ducks and no geese or swans came to the blind. There was nothing for them to do except to talk together or sit dozing in the sun. And, imperceptibly, between them the elements of a pretty intimacy unfolded like spring buds on unfamiliar branches; but what they might develop into he did not know, and she had not even considered.

She had a quaint capacity for sleeping in the sunshine while he was away on the island prowling hopefully after black ducks. And one morning, when he returned to find her asleep at her post, a bunch of widgeon left the stools right under her nose before he had a chance to shoot.

She did not awake. The sun fell warmly upon her, searching the perfections of the childlike face and throat, gilding the palm of one little, sun-tanned hand lying, partly open, on her knee. A spring-like wind stirred a single strand of bright hair; lips slightly parted, she lay there, face to the sky, and Marche thought that he had never looked upon anything in all the world more pure and peaceful.

At noon the girl had not awakened. But something in John B. Marche had. He looked in horrified surprise at the decoys, then looked at Molly Herold; then he gazed in profound astonishment at Uncle Dudley, who made a cryptic remark to the wife of his bosom, and then tipped upside down.

Marche examined the sky and water so carefully that he did not see them; then, sideways, and with an increasing sensation of consternation, he looked again at the sleeping girl.

His was not even a friendly gaze, now; there was more

than dawning alarm in it — an irritated curiosity which grew more intense as the seconds throbbed out, absurdly timed by a most remarkable obligato from his heart.

He gazed stonily upon this stranger into whose life he had drifted only a week before, whose slumbers he felt that he was now unwarrantedly invading with a mental presumption that scared him; and yet, as often as he looked elsewhere, he looked back at her again, confused by the slowly dawning recognition of a fascination which he was utterly powerless to check or even control.

One thing was already certain; he wanted to know her, to learn from her own lips intimately about herself, about her thoughts, her desires, her tastes, her aspirations — even her slightest fancies.

Absorbed, charmed by her quiet breathing, fascinated into immobility, he sat there gazing at her, trying to reconcile the steadily strengthening desire to know her with what he already knew of her — of this sleeping stranger, this shabby child of a poor man, dressed in the boots and shooting coat of that wretchedly poor man — his own superintendent, a sick man whom he had never even seen.

What manner of man could her father be — this man Herold — to have a child of this sort, this finely molded, fine-grained, delicate, exquisitely made girl, lying asleep here in a wind-stirred blind, with the Creator's own honest sun searching out and making triumphant a beauty such as his wise and city-worn eyes had never encountered, even under the mercies of softened candlelight.

An imbecile repetition of speech kept recurring and even stirring his lips, "She'd make them all look like thirty cents." And he colored painfully at the crudeness of his obsessing thoughts, angrily, after a moment, shaking them from him.

A cartridge rolled from the shelf and splashed into the pit water; the girl unclosed her gray eyes, met his gaze, smiled dreamily; then, flushing a little, sat up straight.

"Fifteen widgeon went off when I returned to the blind," he said, unsmiling.

"I *beg* your pardon. I am — I am terribly sorry," she stammered, with a vivid blush of confusion.

But the first smile from her unclosing eyes had already done damage enough; the blush merely disorganized a little more what was already chaos in a young man's mind.

"Has — has anything else come in to the stools?" she asked timidly.

"No," he said, relenting.

But he was wrong. Something *had* come into the blind — a winged, fluttering thing, out of the empyrean — and even Uncle Dudley had not seen or heard it, and never a honk or a quack warned anybody, or heralded the unseen coming of the winged thing.

Marche sat staring out across the water.

"I — am so very sorry," repeated the girl, in a low voice. "Are you offended with me?"

He turned and looked at her, and spoke steadily enough: "Of course I'm not. I was glad you had a nap. There has been nothing doing — except those stupid widgeon — not a feather stirring."

"Then you are not angry with me?"

"Why, you absurd girl!" he said, laughing and stretching out one hand to her.

Into her face flashed an exquisite smile; daintily she reached out and dropped her hand into his. They exchanged a friendly shake, still smiling.

"All the same," she said, "it was horrid of me. And I think I boasted to you about my knowledge of a bayman's duties."

"You are all right," he said, "a clean shot, a thoroughbred. I ask no better comrade than you. I never again shall have such a comrade."

"But — I am your bayman, not your comrade," she exclaimed, forcing a little laugh. "You'll have better guides than I, Mr. Marche."

"Do you reject the equal alliance I offer, Miss Herold?"

"I?" She flushed. "It is very kind of you to put it that way. But I *am* only your guide — but it is pleasant to have you speak that way."

"What way?"

"The way you spoke about — your bayman's daughter."

He said, smilingly cool on the surface, but in a chaotic, almost idiotic inward condition: "I've sat here for days, wishing all the while that I might really know you. Would you care to let me, Miss Herold?"

"Know me?" she repeated. "I don't think I understand."

"Could you and your father and brother regard me as a guest — as a friend visiting the family?"

"Why?"

"Because," he said, "I'm the same kind of a man that you are a girl and that your brother is a boy. Why, you know it, don't you? I know it. I knew it as soon as I heard you speak, and when your brother came into the room that first night with his Latin book, and when I saw your mother's picture. So I know what your father must be. Am I not right?"

She lifted her proud little head and looked at him. "We are what you think us," she said.

"Then let us stand in that relation, Miss Herold. Will you?"

She looked at him, perplexed, gray eyes clear and thoughtful. "Do you mean that you really want me for a friend?" she asked calmly, but her sensitive lip quivered a little.

"Yes."

"Do men make personal friends among their employees? Do they? I ask because I don't know."

"What was your father before he came here?" he inquired bluntly.

She looked up, startled, then the color came slowly back to her cheeks. "Isn't that a little impertinent, Mr. Marche?"

"Good heavens! Yes, of course it is!" he exclaimed, turning very red. "Will you forgive me? I didn't mean to be rude or anything like it! I merely meant that whatever reverses have happened to bring such a girl as you down into this God-forsaken place have not altered what you were and what you are. *Can* you forgive me?"

"Yes. I'll tell you something. I *wanted* to be a little more significant to you than merely a paid guide. So did Jim. We — it is rather lonely for us. You are the first real man who has come into our lives in five years. Do you understand, Mr. Marche?"

"Of course I do."

"Are you sure you do? We would like to feel that we could talk to you — Jim would. It is pleasant to hear a man from the real world speaking. Not that the people here are unkind, only" — she looked up at him almost wistfully — "we *are* like you, Mr. Marche—and we feel starved, sometimes."

He did not trust himself to speak, even to look at her, just at the moment. Not heretofore sentimental, but always impressionable, he was young enough to understand, wise enough not to misunderstand.

After a while, leaning back in the blind, he began, almost casually, talking about things in that Northern world which had once been hers, assuming their common interest in matters purely local, in details, of metropolitan affairs, in the changing physiognomy of the monstrous city, its superficial aspects, its complex phases.

Timidly, at first, she ventured a question now and then, and after a while, as her reserve melted, she asked more boldly, and even offered her own comments on men and things, so that, for the first time, he had a glimpse of her mind at work — brief, charming surprises, momentary views of a young girl's eager intelligence, visions of her sad and solitary self, more guessed at than revealed in anything she said or left unsaid.

And now they were talking together with free and unfeigned interest and pleasure, scarcely turning for a glance at the water or sky, save when old Uncle Dudley made insulting remarks to some slow-drifting gull or soaring bird of prey.

All the pent-up and natural enthusiasm of years was fairly bubbling to her lips; all the long-suppressed necessity of speech with one of her own kind who was not of her own kin.

It seemed as though they conversed and exchanged views on every topic which concerned heaven and earth, flashing from one subject to another which had nothing at all to do with anything yet discussed.

Out around them the flat leagues of water turned glassy and calm as a millpond; the ducks and geese were asleep on their stools; even old Uncle Dudley stood sentinel, with one leg buried in the downy plumage of his belly, but his weather eye remained brilliantly open to any stir in the blue vault above.

They ate their luncheon there together, he serving her with hot coffee from the vacuum bottle, she plying him with sandwiches.

And now, to her beauty was added an adorable friendliness and confidence, free from the slightest taint of self-consciousness or the least blemish of coquetry. Intelligent, yet modest to the verge of shyness, eager yet reserved, warm hearted yet charmingly impersonal with him, he realized that she was finding, with him, only the happiness of speech with mankind in the abstract. And so she poured out to him her heart, long stifled in the abyss of her isolation; and, gazing into his eyes, she was gazing merely toward all that was bright and happy and youthful and responsive, and he was its symbol, God-sent from those busy haunts of men which already, to her, had become only memories of a blessed vision.

And all the while the undercurrent of his own thoughts ran on unceasingly: "What can I do for her? I am falling in love — in love, surely, hopelessly. What can I do for her — for her brother — her father? I am falling in love — in love — in love."

The long, still, sunny afternoon slipped away. Gradually the water turned to pearl, inlaid with gold, then with glowing rose. And now, far to the north, the first thrilling clangor of wild geese, high in the blue, came to their ears, and they shrank apart and lay back, staring upward. Nearer, nearer, came the sky trumpets, answering faintly each to each — nearer, nearer, till high over the blind swept the misty wedge; and old Uncle Dudley flapped his wings and stretched his neck, calling up to his wild comrades of earthly delights unnumbered here under the shadow of death. And every wild goose answered him, and the decoys flapped and clamored a siren welcome; but the flying wedge glided onward through the blue.

"They've begun to move," whispered the girl. "But, oh, dear! It is blue-bird weather. Hark! Do you hear the swans? I can hear swans coming out of the north!"

Marche could not yet hear them, but the tethered swans and geese heard, and a magnificent chorus rose from the water. Then, far away as fairyland, faintly out of the sky, came a new murmur — not the martial clangor of wild geese, but something wilder, more exquisitely unearthly — nearer, nearer, enrapturing its weird, celestial beauty. And now, through the blue, with great, snowy wings slowly beating, the swans passed over like angels; and like angels passing, hailing each other as they winged their way, drifting on broad, white pinions, they called, each to the other in their sweet, unreal voices, gossiping, garrulous, high in the sky. And far away they floated on until they became only a silver ribbon undulating against the azure; and even then Marche could hear the soft tumult of their calling: Heu! Heu! Hiou! Hiou-oo! until sound and snowy flecks vanished together in mid-heaven.

Again, coming from the far north, the trumpets of the sky squadron were sounding; they passed, wedge after wedge, sometimes in steady formation, sometimes like a wavering band of witches, and again in shifting battalions, sternly officered, passing through intricate aërial maneuvers, and greeted by Uncle Dudley and the other decoys with wild beseeching mixed with applause.

Snowy, angelic companies of swans came alternately with the geese; then a whimpering, whispering flight of wild ducks, water-fowl in thousands and tens of thousands, rushing onward through the aërial lanes.

But none came to the blind. Occasionally a wedge of geese wavered, irresolute at the frantic persuasions of Uncle Dudley, but their leader always dragged them back to their course, and the sagging, hesitating ranks passed on.

Sometimes, in a nearer flight of swans, some long-necked, snowy creature would bend its head to look curiously down at the tethered swans on the water, but always they continued on, settling some two miles south of Foaming Shoals, until there was half a mile of wild swans afloat there, looking like a long, low bank of snow, touched with faintest pink by the glow of the westering sun.

IV

Marche, pacing the shabby sitting room after supper, an unlighted cigarette between his fingers, listened to Jim recite his Latin lesson.

"*Atque ea qui ad efeminandos animos pertinent important,*" repeated the boy; and Marche nodded absently.

"Do you understand what that means, Jim?"

"Not exactly, sir."

Marche explained, then added smilingly: "But there is nothing luxurious to corrupt manhood among the coast marshes down here. Barring fever and moccasins, Jim, you ought to emerge, some day, into the larger world equipped for trouble."

"I shall go out some day," said the boy.

Marche glanced up at the portrait of the boy's mother in its pale-gilt oval. Near it, another nail had been driven, and on the faded wall paper was an oval discoloration, as though another picture had once hung there.

"I wish I might see your father before I go North," said Marche, half to himself. "Isn't he well enough to let me talk to him for a few minutes?"

"I will ask him," said the boy.

Marche paced the ragged carpet until the return of Jimmy.

"Father is sorry, and asks you to please excuse him," he said.

Marche had picked up the boy's schoolbook and was looking at the writing on the flyleaf again. Then he raised his head, eyes narrowing on the boy as though searching for some elusive memory connected with him — with his name in the Latin book — perhaps with the writing, which, somehow, had stirred in him, once more, the same odd and uncomfortable sensation which he had experienced when he first saw it.

"Jim," he said, "where did you live when you lived in New

York?"

"In Eighty-seventh Street."

"West?"

"Yes, sir."

"Do you remember the house — the number?"

"No, sir."

"Was it a private house?"

"I don't know. It was very tall. We lived on one floor and used an elevator."

"I see. It was an apartment house."

The boy stood, with blonde head lowered, silently turning over the leaves of an old magazine.

Marche walked out to the porch; his brows were bent slightly inward, and he bit the end of his unlighted cigarette until the thing became useless. Then he flung it away. A few stars watched him above the black ramparts of the pines; a gentle wind was abroad, bringing inland the restless voice of the sea.

In Marche's mind a persistent thought was groping in darkness, vainly striving to touch and awaken memories of things forgotten. What was it he was trying to remember? What manner of episode, and how connected with this place, with the boy's book, with the portrait of his mother in its oval frame? Had he seen that portrait before? Perhaps he had seen it here, five years ago; yet that could not be, because Herold had not been here then.

Was it the writing on the flyleaf that had stirred some forgotten memory? It had seemed to him familiar, somehow — yet not like the handwriting in Herold's business letters to him. Yet it *was* Herold's writing — "Jim, from Daddy" — that was the inscription. And that inscription had riveted his attention from the first moment he saw it.

Who was Herold? Who was this man whose undoubtable breeding and personal cultivation had stamped his children with the same unmistakable distinction?

Somehow or other there had been a great fall in the world for him — a terrible tumble from higher estate to land him here in this desolation of swamp-bound silence — here where only the dark pines broke the vast sky line, where the only sound was the far rumor of the sea. Sick, probably with coast fever, poor, dependent, no doubt, on the salary Marche paid him, isolated from all in the world that made the world endurable to intelligence, responsible for two growing children — one already a woman — what must be the thoughts of such a man on a night like this, for instance?

"I want to see that man," he kept repeating to himself. "I want to see him; and I'm going to."

Restless, but now always listening for the sound of a light tread which he had come to know so well — alas! — he began to walk to and fro, with keen glances toward the illuminated kitchen window every time he passed it. Sometimes his mind was chaotic; sometimes clear. The emotions which had awakened in him within the week were complex enough to stagger a more intelligent man. And Marche was not a fool; he was the typical product of his environment — the result of school and college, and a New York business life carried on in keenest competition with men as remorseless in business as the social code permitted. Also, he went to church on Sundays, read a Republican newspaper, and belonged to several unexceptionable clubs.

That was the kind of a man he had been only a week ago — a good fellow in the usual sense among men, acceptable to women, kind hearted, not too cynical, and every idea in his head modeled upon the opinions he heard expressed in that limited area wherein he had been born and bred.

That was the kind of a man he had been a week ago. What was he now — tonight — here in this waste corner of the world with the light from a kitchen window blazing on him as though it were the flashing splendor streaming through the barred portals of paradise? Was it possible that he, John Benton Marche, could be actually in love — in love with the daughter of his own game warden — with a girl who served him at supper in apron and gingham, who served him further in hip boots and ragged jacket — this modern Rosalind of the marshes, as fresh and innocent, as modest and ardent, as she of the Arden glades?

The kitchen door opened, and Molly Herold came down the steps and straight toward him, unthinkingly, almost instinctively, laying her hands in his as he met her under the leafless China tree in the yard.

"I was longer than usual tonight," she said, "trying to soften my hands with that cold cream you so kindly sent for." She lifted them in the starlight with a little laugh. "They're a trifle better, I think," she said, "but they're always in water, you know, either there," she glanced around at the kitchen, "or yonder with the decoys. But thank you all the same," she added brightly. "Are you going to have another delightful talk, now?"

"Do you care to?"

"Of course. The idea of my not caring to talk to you," she said, laughing at the absurdity. "Shall we go into the sitting room, or walk in the starlight? There are no snakes out, yet," she assured him, "though if this weather holds, the moccasins will come out."

"We'll walk down to the shore," he said.

"One moment, then." She turned and sped to the house, reappearing, after a few minutes, wearing her ragged shooting coat.

"Is your father comfortable?" he asked.

"Yes, thank you."

"Do you think he might want you?"

"No. Jim sleeps next to him, and he is preparing for bed, now." She smiled. "What a darling my brother is, isn't he, Mr. Marche?"

"He's a fine boy."

They moved on together, down the rutted lane, between dismantled fences and ragged, leafless hedges. She was lithe and light and sure footed, but once or twice, as they skirted puddles, he supported her; and the touch of his hand on her body almost unnerved him. Never had he dreamed that contact with any woman could so thrill, so exquisitely shock. And every instant he was falling deeper and deeper in love with her. He knew it — realized it — made no effort to avoid it, fight it off, control it. It was only his speech and manner that he held desperately under bit and curb, letting his heart go to everlasting smash and his reason run riot. And what on earth would be the end he could not imagine, for he was leaving for the North in the morning, and he had not yet told her.

As they came out upon the shore, the dory loomed up, beached, a dark silhouette against the starlit water. She laid her hands on the stern and vaulted lightly to her perch, sliding along to make room for Marche.

From far away in the sound came the confused murmur of wild fowl feeding. Except for that, and the ceaseless monotone of the outer sea, there was no sound, not even the lap of water against the bow.

Marche, who had been leaning forward, head bent as though watching the water, turned to the girl abruptly. "I want to do something for — Jim," he said.

The girl looked up at him, not understanding.

"Will your father let me?"

"I don't know what you mean."

"I mean that I want to send him to a good school — a good boys' school in the North."

She caught her breath, was silent for a moment, then, amazed: "*Would* you do that? Oh, I've wished for it — dreamed of it! But — how can you? You are so kind — so good to us — but how could we — accept?"

"That's why I want to see your father."

"For *that*! Was it really for that, Mr. Marche?"

"Yes — partly." He swallowed and looked the other way, for the girl's excited face was very near his own as she bent forward to search his eyes for the least change of expression — bent nearer as though to reassure herself that he meant it seriously. For an instant her soft breath made the night air fragrant; he felt it, faint and fresh on his cheek, and turned sharply, biting his lips lest he lose all self-control.

"Could you and your father spare him?" he asked carelessly.

"Oh, if you only would give him that chance!" she cried. "But — tell me — *how* can we accept such a thing of you? Is it possible?"

"Would *you* accept it?" he asked, turning toward her.

The question startled her. She looked at him, striving to think clearly, trying to see this offered miracle through calm, impartial eyes.

"I — I would do anything — almost — for Jim," she said. "I'd have no pride left, if his chances lay in the balance. But men — my father — may be different."

He said slowly: "Suppose I offered the same chance to you?"

"What!" she said crisply.

"Suppose I offered you a college finishing, Miss Herold. Would you accept?"

She slowly grew scarlet under his gaze. "That would be insulting," she said, in a low voice.

"Why, when only kindness is meant — as I mean it for Jim?"

"It is not the same. I am a grown woman capable of caring for myself. Such an offer, however kindly meant, could only hurt me, humiliate me — and — I thought you found me companionable as I am. Friends do not offer to better each other — in such a way."

"I have not offered it to you, Miss Herold."

She looked up, still flushed and brilliant eyed; then her face changed softly. "I know it. I was foolishly sensitive. I know you couldn't offer such a thing to me. But I wish I knew whether we could accept for Jim. He is such a darling — so intelligent and perfectly crazy for an education. I've saved a little — that's why I wanted you to hire me for your bayman. You see I don't spend anything on myself," she added, with a blush.

Marche was fighting hard for self-restraint; he was young and romantic, and his heart was very full. "What I'd like to do," he said, "would be to send Jim to some first-rate school until he is ready for college. Then I'd like to see him through college, and, if he cared for it, start him with me in business."

"Oh," she cried softly, "is it possible! Is there — can any man really do such heavenly things? Have you any idea what you are saying? Do you realize what you are doing to me — with every word you utter?"

"What am I doing to — to you?" he asked unsteadily.

"Making me your slave," she said, in a low voice, thrilling with generous passion. "Even for the thought — even if father will not accept — what you have said to me tonight has put me in your debt forever. Truly — truly, I know what friendship is, now."

She clasped her hands tightly and said something else, sweetly incoherent; and, in the starlight, Marche saw the tears sparkling on her lashes.

With that he sprang nervously to the shore and began to tramp up and down the shingle, his mind in a whirl, every sense, common or the contrary, clamoring for finality — urging him to tell her the truth — tell her that he loved her, that he wanted her — her alone, out of all the world of women — that it was for love and for her, and for love of her, that he offered anything, did anything, thought anything now under the high stars or under the circling sun.

And now, as he tramped savagely to and fro, he realized that he had begun wrong; that he should have told her he loved her first of all, and then acted, not promised.

Would she look on his offer scornfully, now? Would she see, in what he asked of her, a bribe desired for the offer he had made in her brother's behalf? She did not love him. How could she, in a week? Never had there been even a hint of sentiment between them. What would she think — this young girl, so tranquilly confident in her friendship for him — what would she think of him and his love? He knew there was nothing mercenary or material in her character; he knew she was young, sweet tempered, reticent concerning herself, clean hearted, and proud. How could he come blundering through the boundaries of her friendship with such an avowal, at a moment's notice?

He returned slowly to the boat and stood looking up at her; and he saw that she was smiling down at him in the starlight.

"Why did you start off so abruptly and tramp up and down?" she asked.

He looked up at her. "Shall we walk back, now?" he said.

She extended her hands to him, and he swung her to the beach. For a moment he retained her hands; she looked at him, smiling, thrilling with all that he had said, meeting his eyes frankly and tenderly.

"You are like some glorious magic prince to me," she said, "appearing among us here to win our hearts with a word."

"Have I won yours with what I have said?"

"Mine? Oh, don't you know it? Do you think — even if it doesn't come true — that I can ever forget what you have wished to do for Jim?"

Still holding her hands, he lifted them, joined her fingers, and laid his lips to them. She bent her head and caught her breath in surprise.

"I am going North tomorrow," he said.

For a moment she did not comprehend his words. Then, a trifle dazed, she looked up at him. "Tomorrow?"

"Yes."

"Are you coming back?"

"Perhaps — next year."

"*Next — year!*"

"Do you — find it — a long time?"

Her straight brows bent inward a little, the startled gray eyes became clear and steady. "Of course I knew that you must go — some time. But I had no idea that it would be so soon. Somehow, I have thought of you as being — here —"

"Do you care?"

Her honest eyes widened. "Care?" she repeated.

"Yes. How greatly do you care?"

The straight brows contracted still more as she stood considering him — so close that the fresh and subtle youth of her freshened the night again with its faint perfume.

Again he touched her hands with his lips, she watching him palely, out of clear, gray eyes; then, as they turned away together, he encircled her slender waist with his arm.

That she was conscious of it, and not disturbed by it, was part of her new mystery to him. Only once, as they walked, when his circling clasp tightened, did she rest her own hand over his where it held her body imprisoned. But she said nothing; nor had he spoken when the belt of pines loomed against the stars once more.

Then, though neither had spoken, they stopped. He turned to face her, drew her into his arms, and the beating of his heart almost suffocated him as he looked into her eyes, clear, unshrinking eyes of gray, with a child's question in their starry depths.

And he answered the question as in a dream: "I love you. I want you for my wife. I want you to love me. You are the first woman I have cared for. All that you are I want — no more than you are. You, as you are now, are all that I care for in the world. Life is young for us both, yet. Let us grow up together — if you can love me. Can you?"

"I don't know."

"Can you not care for me a little, Molly?"

"I do. I know — nothing about — love — real love."

"Can you not imagine it, dear?"

"I — it is what I *have* imagined — a man — like you — coming this way into my loneliness. I recognize it. I have dreamed that it was like this. What is it that I should do — if this is really to come true?"

"Love me."

"I would — if I knew how. I don't know how," she said wistfully. "My heart is so full — already — of your goodness — I — and then this dream I have dreamed — that a man like you should come here and say this to me —"

"Is it in you to love me?"

"I'll try — if you'll tell me what to do — how to show it — to understand —"

He drew her closer, unresisting, and looked deep into her young eyes, and kissed them, and then her lips, till they grew warmer and her breath came fragrant and uneven.

"Can you love me?"

"Yes," she whispered.

"Are you sure?"

"Y-yes."

For a moment's exquisite silence she rested her flushed face against his shoulder, then lifted it, averted, and stepped aside, out of the circle of his arms. Head lowered, she stood there, motionless in the starlight, arms hanging straight; then, as he came to her, she lifted her proud little head and laid both her hands in his.

"Of those things," she said, "that a woman should be to the man she loves, and say to that man, I am ignorant. Even how to speak to you — now — I do not know. It is all a dream to me — except that, in my heart, I know that I do love you. But I think that was so from the beginning, and after you have gone away I should have realized it some day."

"You darling!" he whispered. Again she surrendered to him, exquisite in her ignorance, passive at first, then tremulously responsive. And at last her head drooped and fell on his shoulder, and he held her for a little longer, then released her.

Trembling, she crept up the stairway to her room, treading lightly along the dark entry, dazed, fatigued, with the wonder of it all. Then, as she laid her hand on the knob of her bedroom door, the door of her father's room opened abruptly.

"Molly?"

"Yes, dear," she answered vaguely.

He stood staring at her on the threshold, fully dressed, and she looked back at him, her eyes slightly confused by the light.

"Where have you been?" he said.

"With Mr. Marche."

"Where?"

"To the dory — and back."

"What did he say to you, child?"

She came silently across the threshold and put her arms around his neck; and the man lost every atom of his color.

"What did he say?" he repeated harshly.

"That he loves me."

"What!"

"It is true, father."

The man held her at arm's length roughly. "Good God!" he groaned, "how long has this been going on?"

"Only tonight. What do you mean, father?"

"He tells you that he — he is in love with you? With *you*?" repeated Herold unsteadily.

"Yes. It is true, too."

"You mean he asked you to marry him!"

"Yes. And I said I would."

"*You* love *him*!"

The man's pallor frightened her silent. Then he dropped her arms, which he had been clutching, and stood staring at nothing, gnawing at his colorless lips.

The girl watched him with dawning terror and finally ventured to speak. "Dear, what is the matter? Are you displeased with me? Do you think that he is not a man I should care for? You don't know him, dear. You have only to see him, to speak with him, hear his voice, look into his eyes —"

"Good God!" groaned Herold, closing his sunken eyes. Then, almost feeling his way out and along the dark passageway, he descended the stairs, heavily.

Marche, cleaning his gun in the sitting-room, looked up in surprise, then rose, laying aside stock, fore-end, and barrel, as Herold came into the room. The next instant, stepping nearer, he stared into Herold's face in silence. And so they met and confronted each other after many years.

"Are *you* Herold?" said the young man, in a low voice.

"That is my name — now."

"*You* have been in my employment — for five years?"

"Yes. Judge Gilkins gave me the chance. I could not suppose that the club would ever become your property."

The younger man's face hardened. "But when it did become my property, why had you the indecency to stay?"

"Where else could I go?"

"You had the whole world to — operate in."

Herold's thin face flushed. "It was fitter that I should work for you," he said. "I have served you faithfully for five years."

"And unfaithfully for ten! Wasn't it enough that Vyse and I let you go without prosecuting you? Wasn't it enough that we pocketed our loss for your wife's sake?"

He checked himself in a flash of memory, turned, and looked at the picture on the wall. Now he knew, now he understood why his former associate's handwriting had seemed familiar after all these years.

And suddenly he remembered that this man was Jim's father — and the father of the young girl he was in love with; and the shock drove every drop of blood out of his heart and cheeks. Ghastly, staring, he stood confronting Herold; and the latter, leaning heavily, shoulder against the wall, stared back at him.

"I could have gone on working for you," he said, "trying to save enough to make restitution — some day. I *have* already saved part of it. Look at me — look at my children — at the way we live, and you'll understand how I have saved. But I *have* saved part of what I took. I'll give you that much before you go — before I go, too."

His breath came heavily, unevenly; he cleared his eyes with a work-stained hand, fashioned for pens and ledgers.

"You were abroad when I — did what I did. Vyse was merciless. I told him I could put it back if he'd give me the chance. But a thief was a thief to him — particularly when his own pocket was involved. He meant to send me to prison. The judge held him — he was his father-in-law — and he was an old man with a wife and children of his own."

Herold was silent for a moment, and his gaze became vague and remote, then he lifted his head sharply:

"A man makes one slip like that and the world damns him forever. And I tell you, Marche, that I am not dishonest by nature or in my character. God alone knows why I took those securities, meaning, of course, to return them, as all the poor, damned fools do mean when they do what I did. But Vyse made it a condition that I was to leave the country, and there was no chance of restitution unless I could remain in New York and do what I knew how to do — no chance, Marche — and so fortune ebbed, and my wife died, and the old judge saw me working on the water-front in Norfolk one day, and gave me this place. That is all."

"Why did you feign illness?" asked Marche, in an altered voice.

"You know why."

"You thought I'd discharge you?"

"Of course."

Marche stepped nearer. "Why did you come to me here tonight?"

Herold flushed deeply. "It was your right to know — and my daughter's right — before she broke her heart."

"I see. You naturally suppose that I would scarcely care to marry the daughter of a —" He stopped short, and Herold set his teeth.

"Say it," he said, "and let this end matters for all of us. Except that I have saved seven thousand dollars toward — what I took. I will draw you a check for it now."

He walked steadily to the table, laid out a thin checkbook, and with his fountain-pen wrote out a check for seven thousand dollars on a Norfolk bank.

"There you are, Marche," he said wearily. "I made most of it buying and selling pine timber in this district. It seemed a little like expiation, too, working here for you, unknown to you. I won't stay, now, of course. I'll try to pay back the rest — little by little — somehow."

"The way to pay it back," said Marche, "is to do the work you are fitted for."

Herold looked up. "How can I?"

"Why not?"

"I could not go back to New York. I have no money to go with, even if I could find a place for myself again."

"Your place is open to you."

Herold stared at him.

Marche repeated the assertion profanely. "Damnation," he said, "if you'd talked this way to me five years ago, I'd never have stood in your way. All I heard of the matter was what Vyse told me. I'm not associated with him any more; I'll stand for his minding his own affairs. The thing for you to do, Courtney, is to get into the game again and clean up what you owe Vyse. Here's seven thousand; you can borrow the rest from me. And then we'll go into things again and hustle. It was a good combination, Courtney — we'd have been rich men — except for the slip you made. Come on in with me again. Or would you rather continue to inhabit your own private hell?"

"Do you know what you are saying, Marche?" said the other hoarsely.

"Sure, I do. I guess you've done full time for a first offense. Clean off the slate, Courtney. You and Vyse and I know it — nobody else — Gilkins is dead. Come on, man! That boy of yours is a corker! I love him — that little brother, Jim, of mine; and as for — Molly —" His voice broke and he turned sharply aside, saying: "It's certainly blue-bird weather, Courtney, and we all might as well go North. Come out under the stars, and we'll talk it over."

*****

It was almost dawn when they returned. Marche's hand lay lightly on Courtney's shoulder for a moment, as they parted.

Above, as Courtney stood feeling blindly for his door, Molly's door swung softly ajar, and the girl came out in her night-dress.

"Father," she whispered, "is it all right?"

"All right, thank God, little daughter."

"And — I may care for him?"

"Surely — surely, darling, because he is the finest specimen of manhood that walks this merciless earth."

"I knew it," she whispered gaily. "If you'll lend me your wrapper a moment, I'll go to his door and say good-night to him again."

Her father looked at her, picked up his tattered dressing-gown from his bed, and wrapped her in it to the chin, then kissed her forehead.

So she trotted away to Marche's door and tapped softly; and when he came and opened the door, she put her arms around his neck and kissed him.

"Good night," she whispered. "I do love you, and I shall pray all night that I may be everything that you would wish to have me. Good night, once more — dearest of men — good night."

THE END